W9-CCO-261
McCarty School
3000 Village Green Drive
Aurora, IL 60504
630-375-3407

RIDING *to* WASHINGTON

GWENYTH SWAIN

Illustrated by DAVID GEISTER

3 0022 00502123 K

SLEEPING BEAR PRESS

TALES *of* YOUNG AMERICANS SERIES

ILLUSTRATOR'S ACKNOWLEDGMENTS

I could not have done the paintings in this book without my models,
Todd, Rebecca, Rachel and Emma Syring; Hope Rajacich; Joel Brown;
and the good souls down at Johnson's Barbershop.

Thanks are due to my friend, Aaron Novodvorsky, who chipped in with his usual
helpful advice, found pictures of towel dispensers and took me to The Minnesota
Transportation Museum to look at the great old buses. The dynamic duo,
Mary Schmidt and Charlie Pautler, made me laugh and shared their collection
of magazines, catalogs and original clothing from the time period.

As always, I appreciate the tireless efforts of my dear wife,
Pat Bauer, my loving muse and critic.

Text Copyright © 2008 Gwenyth Swain
Illustration Copyright © 2008 David Geister

All rights reserved. No part of this book may be reproduced in any manner
without the express written consent of the publisher, except in the case of brief
excerpts in critical reviews and articles. All inquiries should be addressed to:

Sleeping Bear Press®
310 North Main Street, Suite 300
Chelsea, MI 48118
www.sleepingbearpress.com

© 2008 Sleeping Bear Press is an imprint of Gale, a part of Cengage Learning.

Printed and bound in the United States.

First Edition

10 9 8 7 6 5 4 3 2 1

Library of Congress Cataloging-in-Publication Data

Swain, Gwenyth, 1961-
Riding to Washington / written by Gwenyth Swain ;
illustrated by David Geister.
p. cm.
Summary: "A young white girl rides the bus with her father to the March on
Washington in 1963—at which Dr. Martin Luther King, Jr., would give his
"I Have a Dream" speech. She comes to see that Dr. King's dream belongs
not just to Blacks but to all Americans"—Provided by publisher.
ISBN 978-1-58536-324-7
1. March on Washington for Jobs and Freedom, Washington, D.C., 1963—Juvenile
literature. 2. King, Martin Luther, Jr., 1929-1968. I have a dream—Juvenile literature.
3. Civil rights demonstrations—Washington (D.C.)—History—20th century—Juvenile
literature. 4. African Americans—Civil rights—History—20th century—Juvenile
literature. 5. Children, White—Indiana—Indianapolis—Juvenile literature.
6. Bus travel—United States—History—20th century—Juvenile literature.
I. Geister, David, ill. II. Title.
F200.S93 2008
323.1196'073—dc22   2007046042

To my father, G. Henry Swain, for sharing memories of the ride to Washington. And to my mother, Margaret Coman Swain, for putting up with me and my four sisters at home during that hot, sticky August of 1963.

G. S.

To those who labor for the rights of all humanity.

D. G.

I know why they're putting me on that bus to Washington. It's 'cause I get in trouble.

"Trouble with a capital T," Mama always says. Most times she says it with a smile in her eyes. Other times, like when I slam the screen door by accident and wake up the twins—well, those times I have to look hard to find the smile.

Daddy doesn't want me to go with him on that bus to Washington, but it sounds like I'm going anyhow.

"A whole lot of people are going to hear Dr. King speak," he told Mama one night late when he thought I was sleeping. "I don't like the idea of taking Janie. She's a spitfire."

You know what *spitfire* means? I think it must mean I spit fire. Guess that's Daddy's way of saying I'm trouble.

"Honey," Mama told Daddy, "that girl makes more mischief than I can bear, what with the twins teething."

So, that's how I ended up riding to Washington, hundreds of miles from home. I knew why I was going, but I wasn't so sure why Daddy was.

We don't have coloreds, or black folks, living in our part of Indianapolis. I don't see many at all, except on TV. Blacks on TV live mostly in the South. They get sprayed at with fire hoses and nipped at by police dogs. But Daddy knows a whole lot of coloreds here from work.

I think that's why Daddy's going to Washington to hear Dr. Martin Luther King speak. Because he thinks we should all work together. But Daddy just says, "We'll see history, Janie. History."

I study history at school, and believe you me it's not exciting. Neither was leaving Indianapolis.

On Tuesday, at the Walker Theatre downtown, a bunch of old buses waited for us. They had names on them like Crispus Attucks School and Rollins Grove AME Church. And everyone getting onto them was dressed like it was the first day of school or Easter Sunday. I figured I was in trouble again, wearing my favorite overalls, but Paul Taylor, from Daddy's painting crew, smiled at me.

"Nice to meet you," said his wife. She had a hat like Mrs. Kennedy wears and a suit to match. "Your overalls look comfy," she said, winking. She was right.

There were old people mixed with young people. Preachers mixed with farmers. And me and Daddy and just a few other whites mixed in with a whole bunch of coloreds. More than I'd ever seen in one place.

I was glad when it was finally time to get on the bus.
I pressed close to Daddy, even in the heat.

We all brought picnic lunches, but by nighttime, we were hungry again. We stopped one, two, three times. Each time Paul Taylor and the driver went inside a restaurant. And each time they came back, shaking their heads.

"No service for mixed crowds," Paul explained.

"Why can't we go in?" I whispered to Daddy. "You and me aren't mixed."

"Would you want to eat where others can't?"

I was so hungry I'd have eaten almost anything, almost anywhere. But maybe Daddy was right. Maybe it was best to stick together. Still, I wondered about the coloreds. They didn't act like troublemakers—and I know a lot about trouble.

To keep our minds off food, Paul Taylor started singing. I stumbled and fumbled over words everyone else seemed to know:

This little light of mine, I'm gonna let it shine.
This little light of mine, I'm gonna let it shine...

We drove across farm fields and through cities, over rivers and mountains. The roll of the wheels put me to sleep until we lurched to a stop. We were at a gas station. Daddy's watch said it was nearly midnight.

Mrs. Taylor walked to the front to ask the driver a question. I only heard his answer. "No, Ma'am," he told her. "I can't let you off here."

She stared at the sign over the restroom door. "No Coloreds" it read. She sniffed in disgust. "I'm going," she said.

Her voice made me rise to my feet. Suddenly, I needed to go, too.

"Sir," I told the driver, "I got to go."

"You could be getting yourself into trouble, young lady," the driver warned.

"I got to go!" I said.

Mrs. Taylor and I walked arm in arm into the station, where a skinny boy not much older than me was trying to stay awake behind a counter. "Young man," Mrs. Taylor said, "we would like the key to the lady's room, please."

Her voice was so strong and clear it woke that boy right up. He looked at one of us, then the other.

"I . . . I can't let you in there," he told Mrs. Taylor. Her arm stiffened in mine.

"Yes, you can," I said.

They both looked down at me, startled.

"Sure," I went on. "It's like my mama and daddy always say, 'You got the choice to do the right thing or not.'" (I didn't say that they usually told me that right after I'd gotten into trouble.)

The boy blinked, confused.

I kept on, like I was talking to a friend. "Mama says I make a lot of wrong choices, but I think letting us in would be the right one now."

The boy's cheeks flushed red. He coughed. Then he looked the other way and shoved the key across the counter, like he'd mislaid it—right in plain sight.

In the bathroom, there was a machine
with a long towel looping out of it.
I reached up to yank on it as hard
as I could to see how much towel
was inside, but I stopped short.
Mrs. Taylor gave me a look while
she straightened her hat.

Mr. Taylor was singing as we pulled
back onto the road:

> *Get on board, children, children!*
> *Get on board, children, children!*
> *Get on board, children, children!*
> *Let's fight for human rights!*

This time, the words made sense and
I sang along.

When we took the key back, our thank-yous overlapped. The boy tried to look busy. He didn't have a "you're welcome" to spare for us.

It was just getting light when we finally parked in a field. Never in my life had I seen so many buses. It was like the biggest basketball tourney you could imagine, only we were all rooting for the same team.

"Morning," Mrs. Taylor called to me as we left the bus.

"Fine weather," Daddy said to no one in particular.

None of us looked like we'd been riding on a bus for a day and a night. We all looked as if we'd just woken up to a day we'd been dreaming about.

Later, when Dr. King was speaking, we all stood together in a group. We were miles away from the podium, but would you believe it? I was sure he was looking right at me.

Dr. King's speech sounded fine. The way he said it was just like music. But I wondered to myself: why is he telling me about his dream? What's it got to do with me?

Then I felt a hand resting soft on my shoulder. Mrs. Taylor gazed at me, tears streaming down her face. And that's when I knew it: that the dream belonged not just to Dr. King and Mrs. Taylor and her husband, but to me and Daddy, and maybe even to that boy at the gas station, too.

AUTHOR'S NOTE

The buses began arriving just after daybreak on August 28, 1963. They parked in long lines, bumper nudging bumper, windows cracked open to let in a breeze. It was going to be a hot, muggy day. The thousands of people who got off the buses weren't too concerned about the heat. Even though many hadn't slept much the night before, they weren't especially tired. The way my father remembers it, the mood was festive, and "there was a feeling of peace."

My father and grandfather, both white men from south-central Indiana, rode the bus to Washington to hear Dr. Martin Luther King, Jr., and others speak on that August day. I was only two years old at the time, but I have long wondered what it might have been like to be a child at the great March on Washington.

In the history books, the March on Washington is best remembered for Martin Luther King, Jr.'s, historic "I Have a Dream" speech. But those who arrived by bus had already made history before King stood before the crowd of over 200,000 at the Lincoln Memorial. The moment they boarded buses in Indianapolis, Memphis, Chicago, and other cities across the country, these people—black and white, Christian, Muslim, and Jew—had begun to realize a dream of coming together in peace. And on that morning in Washington, D.C., they and their dream arrived.